Contents

Edited by Belinda Gallagher

ISBN 0 86112 673 4
© Brimax Books Ltd 1990. All rights reserved.
Published by Brimax Books Ltd, Newmarket, England 1990.
Printed in Hong Kong

My First Storybook

Brimax Books · Newmarket · England

Annie's Basket

by Diane Jackman

It was Annie's birthday. She rushed downstairs to meet the postman. Smiling, he handed her a pile of cards and one parcel.

"I've got a parcel, Mum," shouted Annie. She felt it all over. It was a squashy sort of parcel with no particular shape. Whatever could it be?

She tore off the wrapping
paper.
It was a basket, a plain brown
basket.
"Oh," said Annie, disappointed.
"Let me see," said Mum.
"That is a very nice basket."
"I suppose so," said Annie,
but secretly she thought it was
a very dull present.

"It's what you put into a basket
that makes it exciting,"
said Mum.
And she was right.
In her plain, brown basket
Annie carried her ballet shoes
to her first ballet class; and she
carried her sandwiches to the
school picnic.

She filled it with strawberries when they went to visit Granny. She filled it with flowers for a flower arranging competition at school and won second prize; and she piled it high with redbrown conkers in the Autumn.

But the most exciting moment came on Christmas Day. Annie awoke to a strange noise in her bedroom. She switched on the light and looked around. At the foot of her bed hung a bulging stocking. Interesting looking packages lay on her bedside chair. But the noise was not coming from there.

It seemed to be coming from the window. Annie jumped out of bed and went to look.
The night before she had left her basket by the window and when she saw what was inside she could hardly believe her eyes.

For curled up inside her plain, brown basket was a fat, stripey kitten making funny little mewing noises as it slept. Just what she had always wanted.

"Mum was right," said Annie. "It's what you put into a basket that makes it exciting."

Freddy Teddy's Eye

by *Lesley Sloss*

"When did Freddy Teddy lose his eye?" asked Jill's mum one afternoon.

Jill took Freddy Teddy from under her arm and stared at his face. He did have one eye missing.

"I don't know. Hasn't it always been like that?" Jill couldn't even remember what the eye looked like, though it probably matched his other brown and yellow one.

"No it certainly has not! As if Santa would bring you a one-eyed Teddy! Let's see if I have a spare eye in the sewing box." Jill's mum opened the cupboard where the box was kept.

Jill held Freddy up to her face and looked closely. There was a little hole where the eye must have been. Perhaps he did look a little sad without it.

Jill's mum was already sorting out a selection of toy's eyes. She held up a blue one. "This should do!" she said and put it on Freddy Teddy's face.

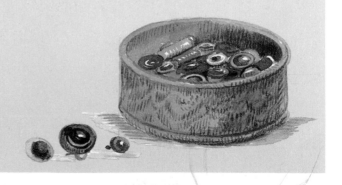

"That looks silly," said Jill.
"It's the wrong colour."
The blue eye was removed and
a brown one put in its place.
"But that's too small! He won't
be able to see properly,"
said Jill.
The next eye was too large,
the next too yellow and the last
one was green.

"I give up," sighed Jill's mum. "Will a button do?"
Jill looked at Freddy. "He says that is the silliest thing he's heard all day," she said.
"Right," said Mum. "I give up, Ask Dad, he might have an idea," and she began putting all the eyes and buttons away.

So Jill asked Dad what to do about Freddy Teddy's eye. "I have just the thing!" said Dad leaping up from his seat and heading for the kitchen. He took Freddy and made Jill face the other way while he looked in the kitchen drawer. Finally he told her to turn around.

"Well, what do you think?" asked Dad.

Freddy was looking very silly.
His missing eye had been
replaced with a bottle top.
Jill tried very hard not to laugh.
"Oh, I see!" said Dad,
pretending to be upset. "Not
good enough, is it? You will
just have to mend it yourself
then."

33

Jill searched the house from top to bottom over the next few days trying to find an eye which suited Freddy and which he felt happy with. On Christmas Eve she gave up.

"Dear Santa," she wrote in her yearly letter, "I would like a doll's pram this year, but I would be even happier if you could find an eye for Freddy, Love, Jill."

She kissed Freddy goodnight and slept as well as she could. When her parents awoke the next day, Jill ran to the sitting room. There was a beautiful doll's pram.

Jill opened lots of presents that day but there was no present for Freddy. Jill tried to cheer him up but he seemed very sad. He didn't even smile until Christmas dinner was ready. It was the crackers that he liked. Jill pulled a cracker for him. Inside it was a yellow hat, a silly joke about a frog and . . . an eyepatch!

Freddy Teddy's one eye opened wide. Then he smiled. Jill put the eyepatch over Freddy's missing eye. When it was in place Freddy sat up very proudly.

He looked very grand.

In Naval Commander Freddy Teddy's eyes, it was the best Christmas present ever!

All Sorts of Noises

by I. Smart

Dogs bark,
Cats meow,
Cows they all say, moo!
Hens cluck
Sheep say, baa!
Owls t'whit t'whoo!

Horses neigh
Goats they say,
Maa, maa, maa;
Babies crying in their prams
Say, whaa, whaa, whaa!

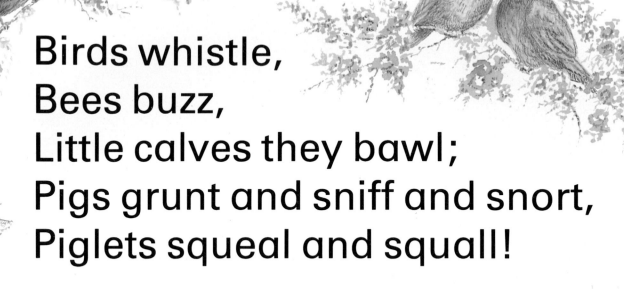

Birds whistle,
Bees buzz,
Little calves they bawl;
Pigs grunt and sniff and snort,
Piglets squeal and squall!

Cocks crow
Ducks quack,
Pigeons say, coo, coo;
But I've never heard a fish
Say anything,
Have you!

Teatime is Four O'clock

by Diane Jackman

"What time is tea-time?"
Biddy Bear asked her mother.
"Four o'clock,"
said Mother Bear.
Biddy ran to tell her brothers.
"Why do you want to know?"
asked Baby Bear, who had
been told once but could never
remember anything for
very long.

"Because tomorrow is Mother's birthday and we are making a special tea for her," said Biddy.

"Then I will set my alarm clock for four o'clock," said Bertie.

"That's a good idea," said Biddy. "Now, let's go and do the shopping."

They bought a big brown loaf and butter, a big jar of honey and a delicious honey cake.

"Mother loves honey cake," said Biddy.
"Everyone loves honey cake," said Bertie.
That night Biddy hid the food in a tin under her bed.
The three little bears slept.
Mother Bear and Father Bear slept, too.
At four o'clock, the alarm went off.

Drrrrrrrrrrr!
Bertie jumped out of bed and
switched it off.
Baby woke up. "Is it tea-time?"
he shouted.
"Ssh," said Biddy and Bertie.
They crept downstairs carrying
the food.

Bertie made a pot of tea, while Biddy cut the bread and buttered it. Then they loaded a big tray with the teapot, the bread and butter, the pot of honey, and the honey cake, with a red candle on top. Very carefully, Biddy carried the heavy tray upstairs to the bedroom where Mother Bear and Father Bear were still sleeping.

Bertie opened the door and Baby rushed in shouting, "Happy Birthday! Happy Birthday!"
Mother Bear and Father Bear sat up in surprise, rubbing their eyes.

"Your birthday tea," said Biddy. She gave Mother Bear the tray.

"What time is it?" said Father Bear.

"It's four o'clock," said Bertie.

"Tea-time," said Baby Bear.

"But it's four o'clock in the morning," said Mother Bear.

"It's still dark outside. Tea-time is at four o'clock in the afternoon!"

The little bears' faces fell.

Then Mother Bear started to laugh, and so did Father Bear. "Never mind," said Mother Bear. "It's a lovely birthday surprise."
"And bears can eat honey cake any time of the day or night," said Father Bear cutting five thick slices.

Mister What's His Name

by I. Smart

There is an imp at our house
Who is always in disgrace,
With blue eyes and curly hair,
A chubby little face.
Whenever things get broken
We all know who's to blame,
It is the imp at our house,
Little Mister What's his name.

He's the one who gave the dog
Our Sunday joint of meat,
Crayoned on the bedroom wall,
Broke the toilet seat;
Put bird seed in the fish bowl,
Teaspoons down the drain,
Scribbled in my storybook,
Broke my yellow plane.

Whatever the imp has done
We love him just the same,
The little imp at our house,
Little Mister What's his name.

David and the Tooth Fairy

by Liz Buckingham

David's tooth had dropped out. He kept it in a safe place until bedtime, then he put it under his pillow.

"Will the Tooth Fairy take my tooth?" David asked his mum as he lay in bed.

"When you're asleep" said Mum. "Then she'll leave you a silver coin."

David felt sure he would never fall asleep. He lay thinking about the Tooth Fairy for ages and ages.

Suddenly, David sat up. He could hear someone speaking. He listened very carefully.

"Oh dear," said a little voice. "What shall I do!"

David switched on his lamp.
Before him was the tiniest
person he'd ever seen. She had
two wings on her back and she
wore a blue dress. Her hair
was golden.
David knew this was the Tooth
Fairy, but how sad she looked.

She sat on David's pillow and put her tiny face in her tiny hands and cried, "I must find the silver coin. I can't go to the Midsummer Ball without it!"
"Can I help!" said David.
"If you're looking for my tooth, it's under my pillow."

The Fairy looked up and said, "I know that, but I've lost the silver coin. It was in my bag when I came in, but now it's gone. I must find it or I can't take your tooth."

"I will help you look for it," said David, "I'll shine my torch under the bed."

David began to search through his toybox. He pulled out the torch and switched it on. "Look! My robot!" said David as he shone the torch under the bed. "And my racing car with the broken wheel. Even poor Teddy is here, with his arm hanging off!"

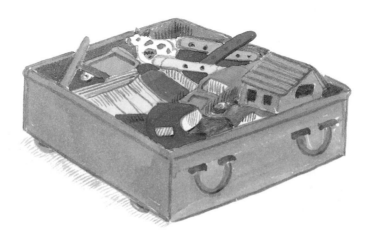

"Hurry up," said the Fairy.
"It will be daylight soon and
we still haven't found the
silver coin."
They searched everywhere in
David's bedroom until David
said, "Come on, we'll look
downstairs."

They crept downstairs with
David shining his torch.
"Can we look outside?"
said the Fairy. "I might have
dropped it there."
"Oh, no," said David. "Mum
and Dad would be very cross
if they knew I'd been outside
at this time of night."

Suddenly, something caught David's eye. "What's that?" he said pointing at the doormat.
The Fairy looked and saw something shiny lying on the floor.
"The coin!" she cried. "We've found it! Oh, thank you, David. Now I can go to the Midsummer Ball."

They crept upstairs again and David climbed into bed.

"Do you want my tooth now?" he asked.

"Oh, no," said the Fairy. "You must be asleep," and she took a tiny silver wand from her bag and waved it in the air. Then she gently touched David's head and his eyes began to close.

When David woke up in the morning, he checked under his pillow. His tooth had gone and in its place was the silver coin. David hurried to show Mum and Dad, then he noticed something strange. On his chest of drawers was his racing car with a brand new wheel and Teddy with a brand new arm.

David smiled. He knew who had fixed his toys and left the silver coin, but he wouldn't tell anyone. Afterall, no one would believe him . . .

Judy

by I. Smart

I don't know how it happens
That I get in such a mess,
A button missing from my coat
And I've torn my dress.
There's glue on my jumper,
A buckle off my shoe,
Ink stains on my fingers,
On my handkerchief too.

I try to keep tidy,
I try to stay clean,
Mum says I'm the messiest
Child she has ever seen.
She simply won't believe me
When I say, "You must see
The other children in my class,
Some are worse than me!"

93